Ladybird Reaaers

Timmy's Tent

To access the audio and digital versions
of this book:

1 Go to www.ladybirdeducation.co.uk
2 Click "Unlock book"
3 Enter the code below

OTlcOH2u3r

Notes to teachers, parents, and carers

The *Ladybird Readers* Beginner level helps young language learners to become familiar with key conversational phrases in English. The language introduced has clear real-life applications, giving children the tools to hold their first conversations in English.

This book focuses on the verb "to have" and provides practice of using "have" and "has" for possession in English. The pictures that accompany the text show an outdoor setting, which may be used to introduce one or two pieces of topic-based vocabulary, such as "garden" and "play", if the children are ready.

There are some activities to do in this book. They will help children practice these skills:

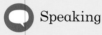 Speaking    Listening*   Writing   Reading   Singing*

*To complete these activities, listen to the audio downloads available at www.ladybirdeducation.co.uk

Series Editor: Sorrel Pitts   **Text adapted by** Hazel Geatches   **Song lyrics by** Wardour Studios

LADYBIRD BOOKS
UK | USA | Canada | Ireland | Australia
India | New Zealand | South Africa

Ladybird Books is part of the Penguin Random House group of companies whose addresses can be found at global.penguinrandomhouse.com.
www.penguin.co.uk   www.puffin.co.uk   www.ladybird.co.uk

 Penguin Random House UK

First published 2021
001

This book is based on 'Learning Time with Timmy', an English language learning experience for pre-school children including the 'Learning Time with Timmy' courses
© British Council 2015; and the 'Learning Time with Timmy' series © Aardman Animations Ltd 2018.

'Timmy Time' and the character 'Timmy' are trademarks used under licence from Aardman Animations Limited.
'Learning Time with Timmy' is a trademark used under licence from Aardman Animations Limited.
britishcouncil.org/english/timmy

Printed in China
A CIP catalogue record for this book is available from the British Library
ISBN: 978-0-241-44007-0

All correspondence to:
Ladybird Books
Penguin Random House Children's
One Embassy Gardens, 8 Viaduct Gardens, London SW11 7BW

Ladybird  Readers

Timmy's Tent

Based on the Learning Time with Timmy TV series
created in partnership with the British Council

Watch the original episode "What's in the Tent?" online.

Picture words

Timmy

Harriet

blanket

sticks

tent

teddy bear

What does Timmy have?
Timmy has a blanket.

What does Timmy have now?
Timmy has some sticks.

Harriet is here. Can she help Timmy?

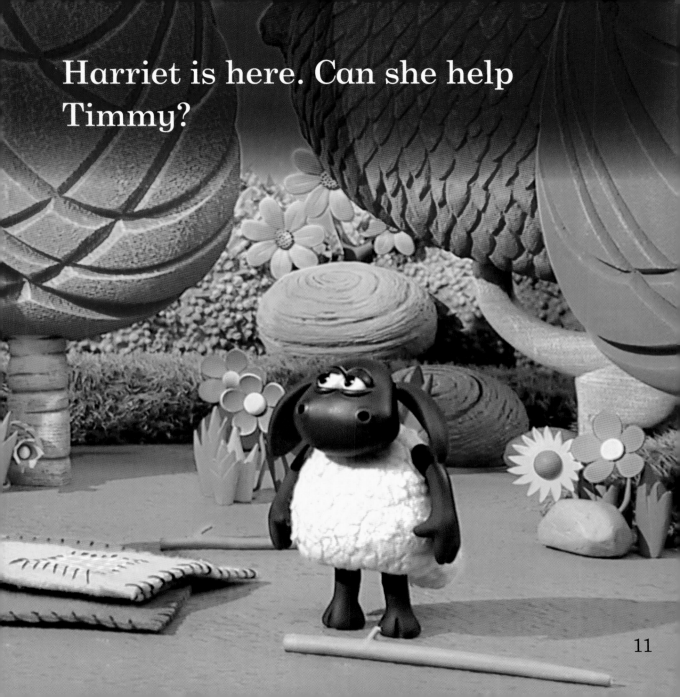

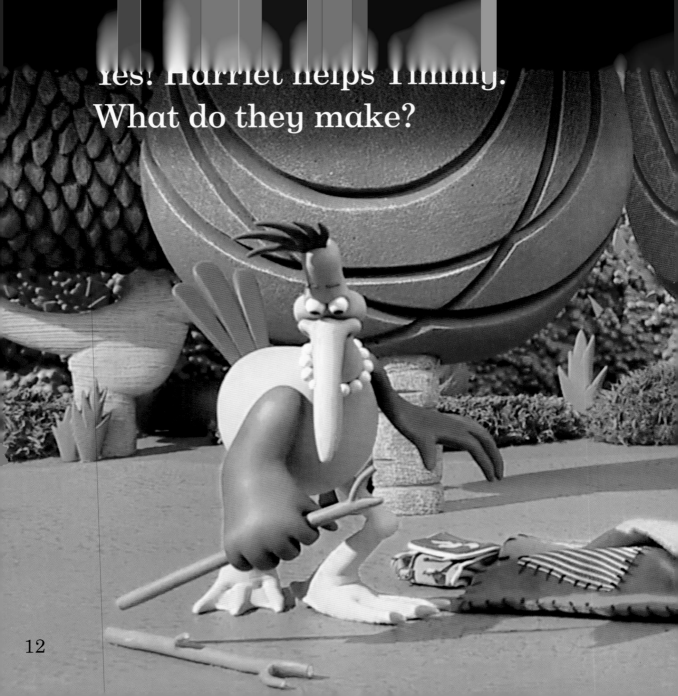

Yes! Harriet helps Timmy.
What do they make?

They have four sticks.

They have a blue and
yellow blanket.

Timmy and Harriet make a tent!

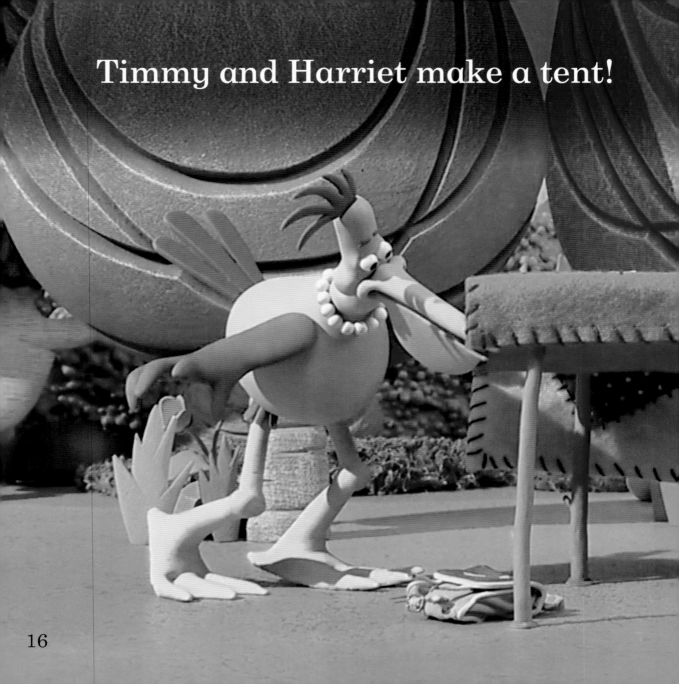

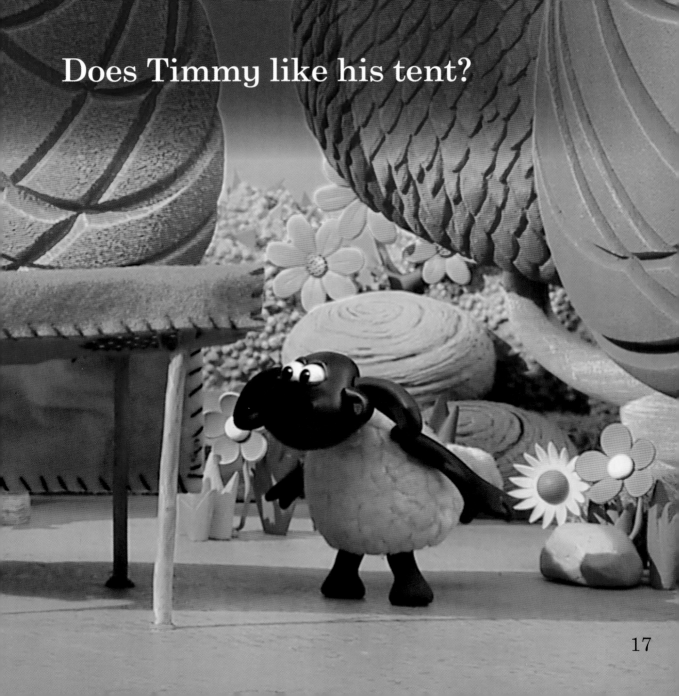

Does Timmy like his tent?

Yes! Timmy likes his tent.

Timmy likes his book and
his teddy bear, too!

Your turn!

1 **Talk with a friend.** 🗨

Hello!

Hello!

What does Timmy have?

Timmy has a blanket . . .

What does Timmy like?

Timmy likes his tent . . .

2 What color? Listen. Circle the words.

1  (orange)   blue

2  blue   red

3  green   brown

4  orange   blue

3 **Listen. Put a** ✓ **by the words you hear.** 🎧

1 a tent ✓

   b blanket ☐

2 a book ☐

   b sticks ☐

3 a help ☐

   b blanket ☐

4 a book ☐

   b teddy bear ☐

22

4 **Listen. Write the first letters.**

1  sticks

2   tent

3   book

5 Sing the song.

What does Timmy have?
Timmy has a blanket!
What does Timmy have?
Timmy has some sticks!

Can Harriet help, Timmy?
Do you like your tent, Timmy? Yes, yes, yes!

What does Timmy have?
Timmy has a book.
What does Timmy have?
Timmy has a bear.

Can Harriet help, Timmy?
Do you like your tent, Timmy? Yes, yes, yes!